The True Adventure of
DANIEL HALL

DIANE STANLEY

PUFFIN BOOKS

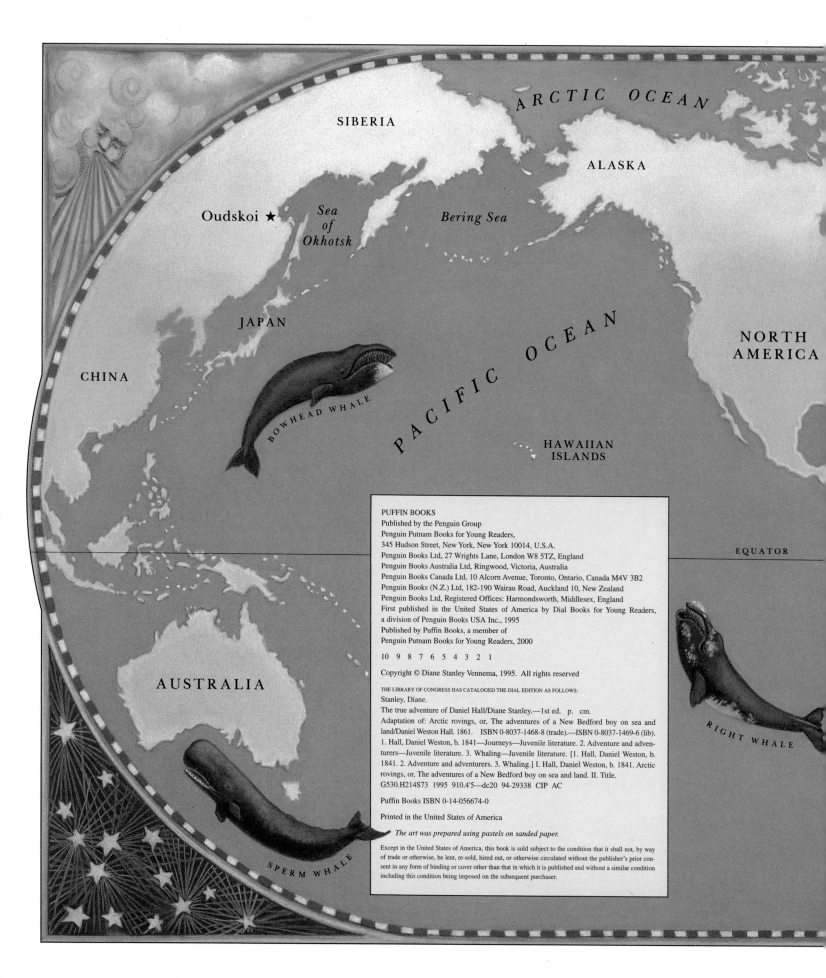

ARCTIC OCEAN

SIBERIA

ALASKA

Oudskoi ★   *Sea of Okhotsk*   *Bering Sea*

JAPAN

NORTH AMERICA

CHINA

BOWHEAD WHALE

PACIFIC OCEAN

HAWAIIAN ISLANDS

EQUATOR

RIGHT WHALE

AUSTRALIA

SPERM WHALE

PUFFIN BOOKS
Published by the Penguin Group
Penguin Putnam Books for Young Readers,
345 Hudson Street, New York, New York 10014, U.S.A.
Penguin Books Ltd, 27 Wrights Lane, London W8 5TZ, England
Penguin Books Australia Ltd, Ringwood, Victoria, Australia
Penguin Books Canada Ltd, 10 Alcorn Avenue, Toronto, Ontario, Canada M4V 3B2
Penguin Books (N.Z.) Ltd, 182-190 Wairau Road, Auckland 10, New Zealand
Penguin Books Ltd, Registered Offices: Harmondsworth, Middlesex, England
First published in the United States of America by Dial Books for Young Readers,
a division of Penguin Books USA Inc., 1995
Published by Puffin Books, a member of
Penguin Putnam Books for Young Readers, 2000

10 9 8 7 6 5 4 3 2 1

Copyright © Diane Stanley Vennema, 1995. All rights reserved

THE LIBRARY OF CONGRESS HAS CATALOGED THE DIAL EDITION AS FOLLOWS:
Stanley, Diane.
The true adventure of Daniel Hall/Diane Stanley.—1st ed. p. cm.
Adaptation of: Arctic rovings, or, The adventures of a New Bedford boy on sea and
land/Daniel Weston Hall. 1861.   ISBN 0-8037-1468-8 (trade).—ISBN 0-8037-1469-6 (lib).
1. Hall, Daniel Weston, b. 1841—Journeys—Juvenile literature. 2. Adventure and adventurers—Juvenile literature. 3. Whaling—Juvenile literature. [1. Hall, Daniel Weston, b.
1841.] 2. Adventure and adventurers. 3. Whaling.] I. Hall, Daniel Weston, b. 1841. Arctic
rovings, or, The adventures of a New Bedford boy on sea and land. II. Title.
G530.H214S73 1995 910.4'5—dc20 94-29338 CIP AC

Puffin Books ISBN 0-14-056674-0

Printed in the United States of America

The art was prepared using pastels on sanded paper.

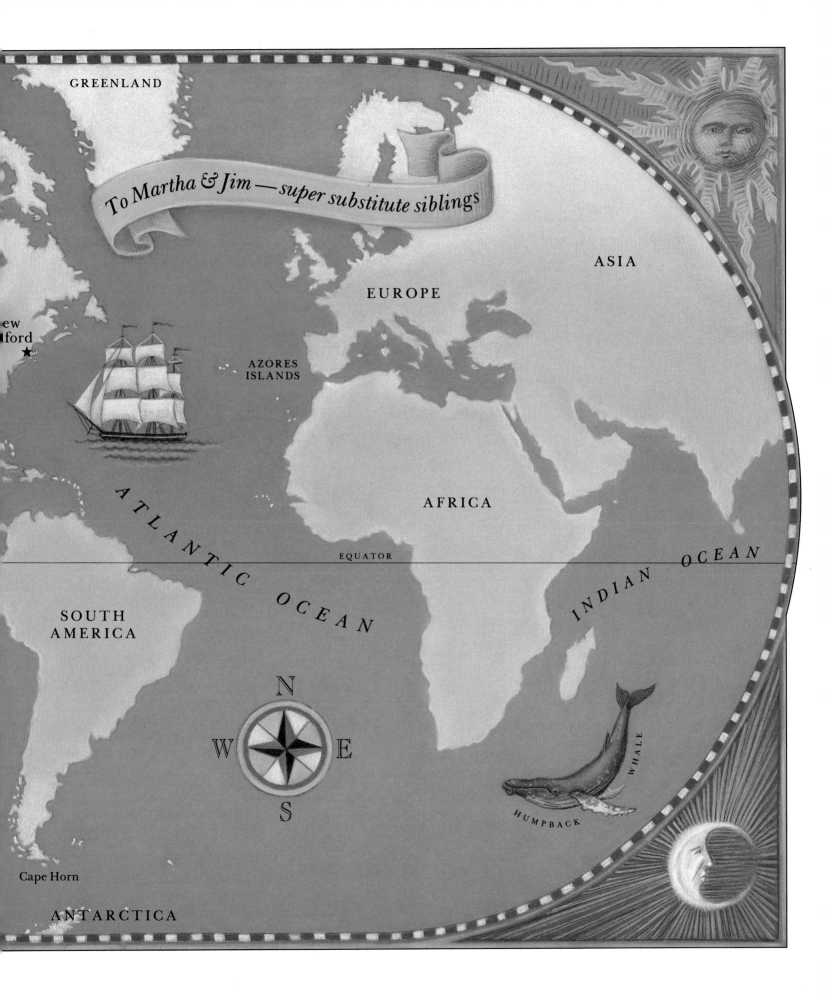

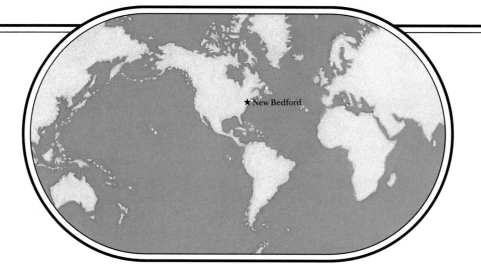

★ New Bedford

This is a true story. Its hero is a boy named Daniel Weston Hall, who went to sea at the age of fourteen. His journey would take him halfway around the world and bring him more danger and excitement than most people see in a lifetime.

Daniel was born in 1841, and he lived in New Bedford, Massachusetts. In those days New Bedford was one of the great whaling towns of the world, and its fine harbor was busy with the comings and goings of Yankee whaling ships.

Everybody in New Bedford knew someone who had been on a whaling voyage. A few came home rich enough to build mansions and keep carriages. But all of them had stories to tell that would turn the head of any boy with spunk and imagination— and Daniel had plenty of both. He wanted to see the wonders they talked about: erupting volcanoes, giant turtles, cannibal islands, and mountains of ice. He longed to test his courage and have adventures. In short, he wanted to be a whaler.

It was not unusual for boys even younger than Daniel to leave home for a ship-board life. Whaling was a respectable career, with the chance of becoming a captain someday. But it was not the career that Daniel's father had planned for his son. William Hall wanted to keep Daniel close to home, for the boy's mother had recently died, and his older brother was already at sea on a merchant ship. His father hoped Daniel would stay right there in New Bedford and work in a store. Yet he could see that the boy was bored by the work, and he wanted Daniel to be happy.

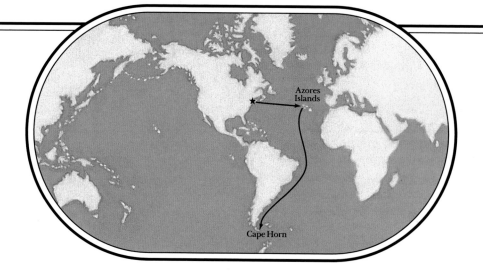

At last William Hall agreed to his son's wishes. Together they went to see a ship's agent, and Daniel signed on for a whaling voyage of three years on the ship *Condor*.

A week later Daniel carried his clothes and bedding into the dark, airless forecastle of the *Condor,* so different from his clean and sunny room at home. For three years he would share that small room with more than twenty other sailors, sleeping amid the damp smell of their sweaty bodies and the sound of their droning snores.

The *Condor* left New Bedford on August 7, 1856, just four days before Daniel's fifteenth birthday. He settled easily into shipboard life, working hard to learn the many complex chores a sailor had to do. And he soon made friends, for there were other young men on board. The older sailors were kind to Daniel, and though many of them were rough characters, Daniel thought them manly and brave. He loved to listen to their lively songs and tales of adventure.

By September the crew had sailed all the way to the Azores Islands without seeing a single whale. Once there had been plenty of whales in those waters. New Englanders had captured them within sight of their church steeples. Now there were fewer and fewer of the giant creatures in the Atlantic. So the *Condor,* like hundreds of other whaling ships, had to make the dangerous trip around Cape Horn—on the southernmost tip of South America—into the Pacific Ocean.

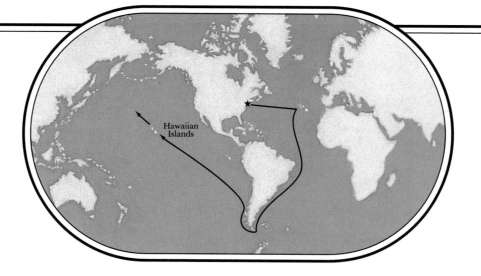

Hawaiian
Islands

Sailors dreaded "rounding the Cape," for it was always dangerous. Fierce storms raged there, even in summer, and many ships had gone down in that icy realm. But the *Condor* survived the difficult passage, then headed north into the Pacific. As the ship neared the equator, the winds grew warm. The men put away their heavy clothes and began to dream of the tropical islands where they would stop to take on supplies.

But the stops were brief, and as they continued north toward the Arctic whaling grounds, the balmy weather soon faded. With each passing day the crew became more discouraged, for they had now been at sea ten months and not a single barrel of whale oil sat in the ship's hold. Even the food was disgusting, and always the same —hard biscuit, salt-cured meat, and stale coffee, called "hot, wet, and dirty."

Daniel was miserable for all these reasons. But he had another problem that troubled him deeply. The captain of the *Condor,* Samuel Whiteside, was a stern man with a hot temper—and he seemed to have taken a particular dislike to Daniel. When the captain was angry, he grew violent and used shocking language. Young Daniel had been gently raised by loving and religious parents, and it was unthinkable to him that he had fallen into the power of such a crude and frightening man.

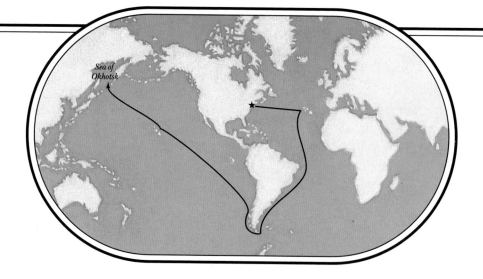

Sea of
Okhotsk

Now the *Condor* neared the Okhotsk Sea, off the coast of Siberia, and the air grew bitterly cold. Still, from the first light of morning until it grew too dark to see, a lookout was always kept from atop the main mast to search for whales. Whenever Daniel's turn came, he felt a wild hope that he might be the first to see the dark back and airy spout of a whale. Squinting his eyes against the stinging winds, and holding on tight as the ship rolled, Daniel would gaze out across the vast expanse of ocean. But he did not see a whale, and neither did anyone else.

And then, on a brisk June morning, their luck turned. From the masthead came the throaty cry, "There she blows!" With astonishing speed the crew began lowering the whaleboats, and within minutes they were rowing frantically in the direction of the spout. It was a short and successful chase, and two hours later the whale's huge carcass was chained to the hull of the ship.

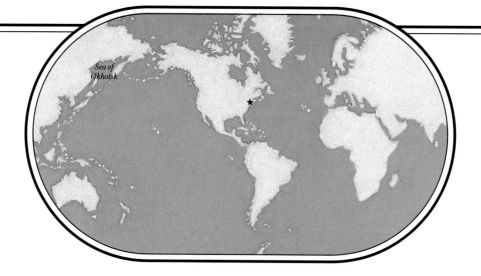

Hunting whales was not always that easy. Once the whale was harpooned, it would often dive deep under the water, dragging the boat's line with it. Minute by minute the men would wait, wondering whether the line would run out. If so, they would have to cut it quickly, or the boat would be pulled under. Then again, the whale might breach suddenly, anywhere—even right under the boat. Many a whaleboat was sunk that way, and though the men were often rescued, others drowned or were killed by sharks.

If the whale was harpooned before it had filled its lungs with air, it could not dive. Instead, it would take off at a run, dragging the little boat behind it at a frightening speed. Whalers called this a "Nantucket sleigh ride," and though it was exciting, it was also very dangerous.

When the whale was completely exhausted, the whalers would approach it for the kill. It was the privilege of the highest-ranking man in the boat to strike the death blow. Standing at the bow, he would take his long lance and plunge it into the weakened whale. He knew he had succeeded when the whale's spout turned red with blood.

Then would come the backbreaking work of rowing the enormous prize back to the ship. There, the deck would become a factory for cutting up the blubber, boiling the oil, and storing it in barrels. The smell was dreadful, and the men were soon coated with an oily black film. The deck became a slippery mess of grease and gore.

And how did Daniel feel about this bloody business? It must have seemed perfectly natural to him. In those days people were accustomed to killing animals. They often butchered their own hogs or chickens rather than buying meat from a store. They believed that God had given mankind the free use of all creatures of the earth and sea—and the whale was a very useful creature.

Whalers hunted the baleen whales such as the bowheads, humpbacks, and right whales for both oil and "whalebone." Whale oil was used to light lamps and lubricate machines. "Whalebone" was baleen, the horny plates that hang from a baleen whale's upper jaw and strain out the tiny sea life it eats. Strong and flexible, baleen was the plastic of Daniel's age, used to make corset stays, hoopskirts, and umbrellas.

The sperm whale was also hunted for oil, though not for baleen; it has teeth instead. It was especially prized for the waxy spermaceti found in its head. This made the best candles, smokeless and very bright. Its intestines might also yield a rare lump of ambergris, worth a fortune because it was a key ingredient in fine perfume.

Daniel was like most people of his time: He did not worry that someday all the whales might be gone. To him they were no different than any other wild creature, except that the "blubbery monsters" were bigger and more dangerous.

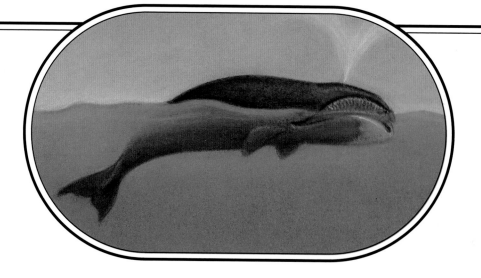

Daniel was busy in the days that followed, for suddenly whales were plentiful.
The men barely had time to eat or sleep and spent every waking hour either catching
whales or processing the blubber. Daniel did his part gladly, for like all the crew, his
pay depended on how much money would be made by the voyage's end. But he also
worked hard because he wanted to stay out of trouble. He had already had one run-in
with the captain, who had seized him with no warning and given him a brutal
beating. Daniel still didn't know what he had done to deserve it.

Then one day Daniel and another boy took to boxing in the forecastle. They were
only pretending to fight, not trying to hurt each other. But the first mate reported
them to the captain, who fell into a screaming rage. He picked up a knotted whip and
gave the boys a dozen vicious blows across their bare backs. Daniel had never imagined
such pain. After that, though his wounds began to heal, the bitterness in his heart
would not go away.

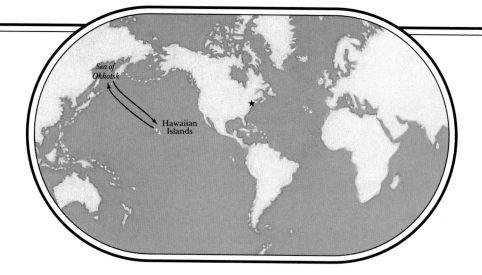

In October the whaling season in the north came to an end, and the *Condor* headed south toward the Hawaiian Islands. There the ship was to take on fresh food and water and be made ready for another season in the Arctic. As they neared the islands, Daniel made a decision. He would go to the captain and ask for a discharge. From Hawaii he would find a ship and work his way back to New Bedford. But he should have known better, for the captain refused to release him.

It was at about this time that Daniel became friendly with a boy he called Elias D. Tolman. (The boy signed on for the voyage under the name of Albert Sherman, and we don't know why he used two names. Perhaps he was a runaway.) Elias, too, hated life on board the *Condor.* Talking to each other gave the boys comfort, and they soon agreed that if they ever got the chance, they would desert the ship.

Once again the ship sailed toward Arctic waters. By the end of April 1858 they were back in the Okhotsk Sea, and Daniel's second whaling season began.

For a while things seemed to go well. Then one day Daniel was assigned to the captain's boat. They were rowing hard in pursuit of a whale when Daniel's oar missed a stroke, slowing the boat. Whiteside again grew wild with rage, knocked the boy off his seat, and began kicking him. Then the captain grabbed an oak stick and beat him so fiercely that Daniel thought he might die.

At last Whiteside threw down the stick in exhaustion and ordered Daniel to get up and row. From that moment Daniel thought of nothing but escape.

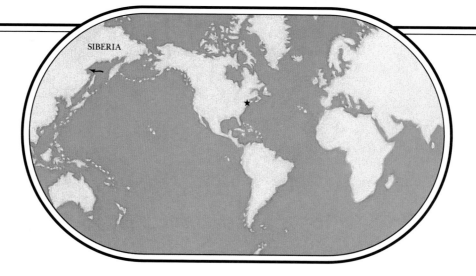

SIBERIA

His chance came only a few days later. It was October, and bitterly cold, when two whaleboats were sent to help bring back a whale that had been captured a long way from the ship. Daniel and Elias were among the crew. The men didn't find the whale till late in the day, and since they were not far from the Siberian coast, they decided to take shelter there for the night and tow the whale back in the morning.

The sailors made a crude hut and built a fire. The boats had been stocked with food, and the second mate had secretly brought some rum. The men ate well and drank till they grew drowsy. And so it happened that Daniel and Elias, who had not had any rum and were still wide awake, were ordered to stand watch over the fire. Their moment had come.

Once all the men were soundly sleeping, the two boys quietly began collecting the things they would need. Into a canvas bag they put some food, tin cups, a compass, matches, two knives, and a pair of ship's pistols with extra ammunition. Daniel knew he was stealing, but he did it only to save his own life.

Then quickly the two boys scurried out into the bitter Siberian night. They had every reason to be afraid, for peril surrounded them. They might die of the cold, or starve, or be killed by wild animals. And if they survived the winter, how could they ever hope to get home from such a remote spot? Yet their hearts were filled with joy. For as Daniel would later write, "We were free!—free from a life of slavery—free from tyranny—free from the oppressive power of our fellow-men."

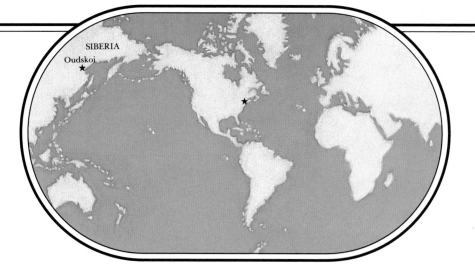

Not far away a small party of Yakut people had built a fishing camp. The boys planned to seek help there, but they knew it was the first place their shipmates would look for them. So for two days they stayed out in the wilderness, building fires to stay warm and keep wild animals away. At last they headed toward the camp.

The Yakuts were a peaceful people. When Daniel and Elias told them in sign language that they had been mistreated on their ship and had deserted, the Yakuts agreed to take them in. Then they sent a message to the nearest village, Oudskoi, asking what should be done with the young Americans.

Oudskoi was a penal colony, a kind of open prison for criminals and enemies of the Russian tsar. Such colonies were in Siberia because it was the coldest and most desolate part of Russia; few people lived in Oudskoi willingly. And it was to that unhappy place that the boys soon learned they would have to go.

Escorted by four Yakuts, Daniel and Elias set out to walk to Oudskoi, a distance of over sixty miles. They had gone about halfway when it began to grow dark. They pitched camp for the night and made a supper of dried fish and horsemeat.

At bedtime they agreed to take turns staying awake to keep the fire going. Daniel's turn came, and as he sat quietly by the fire, watching the flames, his thoughts turned to home. He knew that when the *Condor* reached port, word of his disappearance would be sent to his family. It broke his heart to think how deeply they would suffer. With these sad thoughts Daniel drifted into sleep.

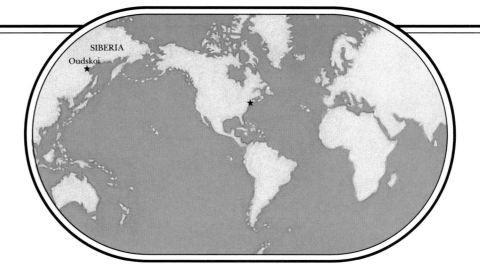

SIBERIA
Oudskoi

While he slept, the fire burned down to ashes, and several bears approached the camp. At the sound of a low growl, Daniel awoke to see the great, shaggy body of a grizzly towering over one of the sleeping men. Daniel screamed, waking his companions, and for a moment the startled bear froze. That gave Daniel just enough time to reach for his pistol and fire. To his astonishment, the huge creature fell.

Quickly, one of the Yakuts began to build a new fire as more bears circled the camp. The other three grabbed their short spears while Daniel and Elias loaded their guns. They had hardly done so when a second bear bounded out of the bushes. It leaped upon them with a roar, snapping the spears and slamming the men onto the ground. This time Daniel only wounded the bear. It attacked with renewed rage, slashing one of the men in the leg with its claws.

Now Elias fired, and the bear staggered backward, then collapsed and lay still. By now the fire was blazing, and the other bears retreated into the night.

No one slept after that. First they tended the wounded man; then they skinned the bears and divided up the meat. When the job was finally done, the Yakuts gathered up the heavy furs and gave them to Daniel and Elias. In the bitter nights ahead, as the boys lay wrapped in their soft bearskins, they would often remember that generous gift of warmth.

The following afternoon they reached Oudskoi, where the boys were brought before the village council. One of the men knew a little English, and he acted as their translator. The council decided Daniel and Elias could share their food and shelter only if they were willing to join in the hard labor to which the convicts had been condemned. Daniel was most willing, but he could not do the work. The beating he had received from the captain had injured his side, causing him terrible pain.

So while Elias was taken into the community, Daniel was not. However, he was given a lonely little hut in which to live. The villagers promised that once a month they would bring him a small portion of horsemeat, dried fish, and rye meal. This food, plus whatever he could get from hunting, would have to feed him through the winter.

The little house was drafty, and there was no way to heat it. So first Daniel filled the cracks in the walls and roof. Then he built a crude fireplace and chimney out of flat stones and clay. Finally he set about furnishing his new home. He built a sleeping platform and covered it with dried leaves for a mattress, putting his bearskin on top. Then he added a table, a couple of stools, a storage box, and some shelves. He made dishes and spoons out of wood, and cups from birchbark. These he put on his shelves with the same pride with which his mother had once displayed her good china. It pleased him to think that he had created the rough image of a New England cottage there in the Siberian wilderness.

But working on the house had made his injury worse. The wound became swollen and throbbed with pain. Daniel felt sure it was infected, but he could do nothing about it. He took to his bed and stayed there, helpless and suffering.

One day the door of his little house swung open, and an old Yakut man came in. He was a stranger, and as Daniel soon found out, he was a medicine man, probably sent there by the villagers. He came over to Daniel and began to probe the wound with expert fingers, nodding his head gravely. Then, before Daniel could object, he brought out a polished bone dagger and lanced the wound. Suddenly the throbbing pain was gone. But the old man had not finished, for now he began to explore the wound with a blunt knife. Moments later he pulled out several splinters of bone. Daniel's ribs had been fractured by Captain Whiteside's violent blows.

Then the old man bandaged the wound carefully and left as quietly as he had come. Within two days Daniel was able to get out of bed, and from that time he felt much better.

Once he was well enough, Daniel began to go hunting in the wilderness beyond Oudskoi to add to his food supply. He set out through the snow one day and had wandered far from home, when he heard the howl of a wolf. Walking into a clearing, he was stunned by the sight of not one wolf, but fifty! They spotted Daniel and ran toward him, howling loudly. To his horror, Daniel heard the answering cry of more wolves. He was surrounded.

Not far behind him stood a tall tree. If he could just get to it in time, he might be safe. So Daniel took aim at the largest wolf, which he thought to be the leader, and pulled the trigger. In the confusion that followed, Daniel reached the tree, grabbed a low bough, and swung himself up out of reach.

Only seconds later the wolves surrounded the tree, snarling. For all the danger he was in, Daniel couldn't help laughing at their disappointed rage. But he soon grew serious again, for he didn't have enough ammunition to fight so many wolves. As they seemed determined to wait him out, Daniel was doomed to stay there all night.

Through the long, dark hours he sat on his hard perch, trying to stay warm and to sleep without falling. When he woke, a cold, gray dawn was showing against the dark forms of the trees. He was stiff with cold, and horribly hungry. And the wolves were still there.

But fortune was kind to Daniel Hall. About midday a large grizzly bear lumbered into the clearing. Realizing its mistake, the bear turned quickly, but it was too late. In seconds the wolves deserted their post under the tree and went after the bear. Daniel leaped from his branch and dashed away toward home.

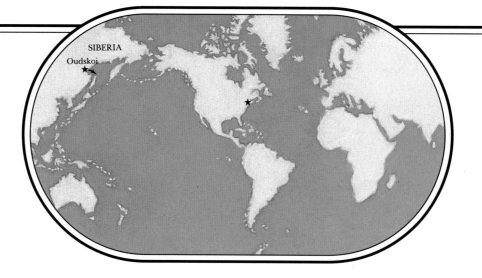

The winter dragged on like nothing Daniel had ever imagined. It lasted for eight months, and from November to February he guessed the temperature to be about forty degrees below zero. In the deepest months of winter, daylight lasted a scant two hours, and there could be eight to ten feet of snow on the ground.

But slowly the days grew longer and warmer. At last the snow began to melt and the first green shoots appeared. Summer had arrived in Siberia. Daniel knew the time had come to leave Oudskoi and travel to the coast, for with the summer would come the whaling ships, his only hope of rescue.

In June 1859 Daniel and Elias began walking east, toward the sea. In less than two days they came in sight of the bay. To their delight they saw that it was filled with ships whose white sails sparkled in the crisp, clean air. As they watched, the boys saw one of the ships turn toward the shore and lower a whaleboat. They could hardly believe it when they saw the boat head straight for the beach.

The boys took off in a run, shouting and waving their arms. They got there just as the boat glided in. Before they could say another word, the mate jumped ashore and loudly asked if one of them was Daniel Hall of New Bedford.

Even in his most hopeful dreams Daniel could not have imagined such a rescue. All he had to do was step into the boat and be rowed back to the ship!

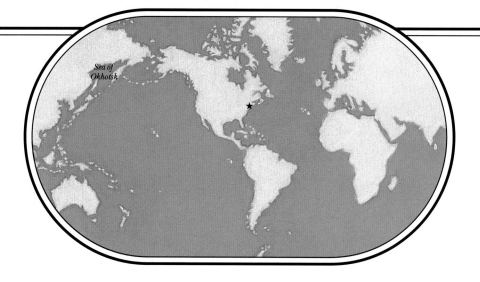

Sea of
Okhotsk

It was here that Daniel and Elias parted. Daniel was taken immediately to the ship *Daniel Wood,* and the next day Elias was taken on another ship to work his way back to America.

Daniel was greeted on board the ship with cheers from the crew and a warm handshake from the captain. They seemed as overjoyed as he was, for they had been searching for him for weeks!

Later he learned how it had all come about. The captain showed him a copy of the *Whalemen's Shipping List,* a weekly publication that was read by sailors all over the world. The captain pointed to a notice that had caught his attention, for it had appeared every week for three months. It begged all sailors cruising in the Okhotsk Sea to be on the lookout for Daniel and Elias, who had been left on that cold and dangerous shore. It was signed, William Hall. From halfway around the world Daniel's loving father had brought about his rescue.

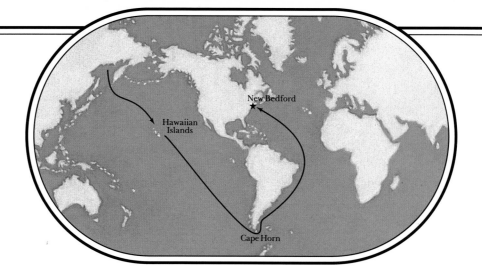

Daniel hurried home as fast as he could go—but unfortunately that was not very fast. The captain of the *Daniel Wood* had taken him on as a crew member, and once more he became a whaler. In fact it took another full year and service on two more ships before Daniel finally caught sight of New Bedford.

As the ship came into the harbor, it was met by a fleet of little boats—friends and relatives who had rowed out to meet them. Daniel caught his breath as he recognized a familiar figure, rowing with the energy of a much younger man. It was his father!

William Hall boarded the ship and frantically began searching for the boy, but all he saw were burly, sunburned sailors. At last he spotted a tall, well-built young man and realized with a shock that it was Daniel, now almost nineteen.

He hurried toward his son. "For several moments," Daniel later wrote, they were both so overcome with emotion that "neither could find voice to speak."

When they came ashore soon afterward, Daniel was given a hero's welcome. Not only were his family and friends gathered there to shower him with tears and kisses, but hundreds of strangers, having heard of his adventure, had come down to greet his arrival with cheer after cheer.

So much had happened since he had left this place and these people. He had known fear and suffering, and faced them with courage. He had seen the world and grown to manhood. And now, with joy in his heart, he was home.

P O S T S C R I P T

Captain Whiteside did not escape punishment for his treatment of Daniel. William Hall brought him to court and he was ordered to pay three hundred dollars in damages. Whiteside was not present for the trial, however, for he was at sea, as captain of the *Emily Morgan*. He obviously had not changed his ways, for when the ship landed in Honolulu, her entire crew refused to sail with him anymore. It was the last ship he would ever command.

We know very little about what happened to Daniel after his return to New Bedford. But it is clear that he never could settle down to life as a clerk. Less than a year after his return he became a Union soldier in the American Civil War, serving in the Massachusetts Third Regiment. He came home safely from that terrible conflict, then left again. When his father died (on Daniel's twenty-third birthday), the court papers listed Daniel as "at sea, whereabouts unknown." We can only imagine what further adventures came his way.

The story of his remarkable voyage has come down to us because he wrote a book about it in 1861 called *Arctic Rovings: or, The Adventures of a New Bedford Boy on Sea and Land*. He dedicated it to his father. Though the book went out of print long ago, it was republished in 1968 in a new edition by Jerome Beatty, Jr., who edited it and added some interesting notes.

Arctic Rovings is a long book, written in the somewhat stilted style that was popular in those days. *The True Adventure of Daniel Hall* is based on *Arctic Rovings*, though I have taken some artistic license in order to shorten and simplify it for younger readers. But nothing of substance has been left out, and at its heart this retelling is the same incredible story that Daniel told over one hundred years ago.

Special thanks to Virginia Adams, Librarian, The Old Dartmouth Historical Society
Whaling Museum in New Bedford, Massachusetts, for her assistance in verifying the facts
in this book, and to Paul Cyr of the New Bedford Free Public Library for his help
in locating certain documents relating to Daniel Hall's life.